Manifest it, Bitch!

USING YOUR INNER BADASS SELF TO ACHIEVE HAPPINESS, FULFILLMENT, AND LOVE

By Mary Mehrkens

First published by That Guy's House, 2020

www.thatguyshouse.com

Copyright © Mary Mehrkens, 2020

ISBN: 978-1-913479-31-2 (Print)

ISBN: 978-1-913479-32-9 (Ebook)

Contents

Foreword

When I met Mary for the first time, we were both assistants somewhere where being an assistant was not a particularly good position. A few weeks after I started, Mary left the company, having found a much better paying – and better in general – job. We reconnected about a year later, and Mary had yet again advanced to a job even better than the last one and gotten engaged to her lovely fiancé, whereas I had washed out of the assistant job and was, to put it lightly, struggling in all other aspects of my life. Of course, I was happy for her because that's just the type of person I am, but I was also furious that she was so much more successful than I was. There were rumblings of Mary's witch-hood at our old job, but I had to know the truth behind the rumors; what was it that gave this woman so much power?

I learned two things very quickly after this. First, Mary is a deeply generous person, almost *too* happy to share her plethora of life secrets and good-vibe-inducing tips. And second, I learned about Manifesting. In a very real way, I am the titular Bitch.

A little about myself; I'm a very result-oriented, objectivity-over-all type of person. I've never believed all that much in "auras" or "spiritual toxins" or anything of the sort, and I would dismiss anything even remotely new age with an eye roll and, if I was feeling particularly dramatic, a derisive snort. This is all to say that when Mary first started tutoring me in the way of focused thinking and all that other stuff, I dismissed it with an eyeroll and a derisive snort. We were still friends though, and over the next few months, as her personal and career desires kept advancing, I realized there was truth in her teachings. There may not have been a double-blind study I could skim, then pretend I read the whole thing, but the proof I needed was right in front of my face; Mary's continued success.

So, Mary began to teach me. I'll skip the lessons she imparted because those make up most of the book you're about to read, but the end result was astounding. Since learning about manifesting, I find my life has a stronger sense of purpose, I feel more prepared to accomplish my goals, my hair's growing back and my pe- okay, it doesn't go that far, but I can't deny Mary has fundamentally changed me for the better. While you won't get the in-person experience I did, you can have the next best thing by turning the page. Lucky you.

Augustus Schiff

This book is dedicated to all the dreamers, skeptics, wanderers, and lovers alike. Whether you know what it is you want in life or not, I designate this advice to you. Take it with you in everyday life. Prosper, thrive, live, love, laugh, and know that The Universe and I are cheering you on.

How To Use This Book

Well, you did it, bitch! You decided that it's time to live the life you were always meant to live through manifestation. Go you! I'm your cheerleader. The Universe is your cheerleader. Both The Universe and I are on your side, and we want the absolute best for you! By opening this book, you've accomplished the first big step in taking control of your life. You hold the reins, truly. Manifestation works! And I'm going to tell you what it is, how to use it, and how to continue to attract the things you want. Because guess what? You can have everything you want through this process.

My 4 Rules For This Book

1. Keep a pen or pencil with you as you read because fun fact... It's also a workbook! A toolkit proceeds each chapter. These manifestation exercises are meant to aid you on this journey.

2. Stay present as you read. For real. Turn off the television. Keep your cell phone far away. If you have

a cat, don't let that cat walk all over the pages. This journey needs your full attention.

3. Read this book sequentially. Every part is important, and it's written in a specific order so that you fully understand the "whats" and the "hows" of this process.

4. Have fun! Seriously. I want you to have fun learning and experiencing manifestation.

The 4 Parts Of This Book

The 4 parts of this book will introduce you to the manifestation process, what tools you can use, how to manifest everyday shit, and what to do when the processes aren't working.

Part 1: What Is Manifestation?

In the first part, I'll go over what manifestation is and what the steps are to manifest your desires.

Part 2: Easy Manifestation Tools

Part 2 is all about the fun tools you can use to up your manifestation game. We'll go over how to create a vision board that actually works, basic witch-y candles, manifesting through visualization, mantras, and how gratitude can attract the things you want into your life more easily.

Part 3: Manifestation In Everyday Life

The third part is about how to use manifestation in everyday life, whether you're trying to attract wealth, love, or experience.

Part 4: What To Do When The Processes Just Aren't Working

In the final part, I'll lay out exactly what you need to do if the manifestation processes aren't working for you. You'll learn what it means to release, accept, and redo this manifestation process, and why you shouldn't get down on yourself if it doesn't work the first time.

Now get that pen or pencil, and let's get started! Are you ready?

Introduction

Today, I'm a comedian, writer, witch, and Pilates instructor living my best life in sunny Los Angeles. I soak up this existence every damn day. I'm grateful, positive, social, and I feel like this is who I was always meant to be. But... way back when, I used to think The Universe was against me, that it was the enemy. When bad things happened, I blamed a higher power. I blamed the world. I blamed external forces. But little did I realize; my thoughts were creating *my reality*. I was the *creator* of what was happening.

Little, naive 20-year-old me got kicked out of my acting program in college, and I thought The Universe hated me. I believed I had negative karma keeping me from living the life I wanted. My life purpose dissolved instantly. I wasn't good enough. Acting wasn't in the cards for me. Though it's not life and death, at the time, it *was*, and my world crumbled. The friends I made were from that acting program. All I had been studying for... it was all leading up to becoming an actor. The moment I was told that "your acting isn't strong enough," my body literally ached from the disappointment. The Universe punished me... or at least I thought it did.

Though I got kicked out of the acting program, I discovered a new path and attended another college after some much needed soul searching... and a lot of self-care (face masks, long baths, wine... you get it). But I still didn't know much about manifestation.

It wasn't until changing my studies in college and graduating, that I discovered manifestation. I, like many millennials, watched *The Secret* a bazillion times and loved this idea that we create our reality. I loved that it was The Universal Law! And the vision boards?!?! Come on! That sounded like such fucking fun! But then I started to explore this "Law of Attraction" stuff more. I created my own rules because they worked! And they worked for other people like me. It was like "the secret" to *The Secret*; some crazy shit that our whole existence is created through our thoughts.

Let me paint a picture; this is you – you're young and desperate. You're stuck, struggling, broke, lonely. Floating around in space with no real direction, feeling like nothing ever works in your favor. And you work! You work relentlessly. You've been told if you work hard, you'll be happy and successful. But then you heard about this manifestation stuff just a little bit. You've turned on Netflix and watched *The Secret* just like me, but you're still confused about manifestation. But once you learn what I've learned, you'll have the tools and knowledge to live out your life purpose, to live the life of your dreams, to take on the world with positivity and joy, and be the master of your own existence!

After reading this book, you'll go from just another negative person who thinks the world is out to get you to a powerful, happy, fulfilled human being. You'll trust The Universe and trust that you're the co-creator of your life, because guess what... *you are*. Before you start, forget everything you know or *think* you know about manifestation. It's best to be open without any prior notion of the process.

Part 1

WHAT IS MANIFESTATION?

In Part 1, we'll go through my 5 basic steps of manifestation. Read with an open mind and absorb the information. Forget what you've learned from other books, movies, podcasts, and start with a clean slate. You'll need these steps as you read on. You'll learn why we do these basic steps, and you'll understand how they work in conjunction with The Universe.

What is Manifestation?

Manifestation is the process of attracting what you want from The Universe – it's also referred to as the "Law of Attraction," but let's just stick to calling it manifestation.

And manifestation is easy. You've manifested things into your life already.

When you look for a job, you imagine it, visualize it, work for it, and get the job. That's manifestation.

When you're hungry, you think of what you want to eat, and you either go out and get food or you cook it. That's manifestation.

So yes, you've manifested things into your life, but here are the steps to do it more clearly and consciously. I want you to do it consistently and refine what you're already capable of.

Most manifestation books say there are 3 steps of manifestation: Ask, believe, and receive. I use 5, and they're super easy:

1. Just Ask The Universe!

2. Fake It 'til You Make it!

3. Release It Like You Just don't Care

4. Inspired Action

5. Receive it, Dude!

Chapter 1

STEP 1: JUST ASK THE UNIVERSE!

When I was a child, believe it or not, I lived on a farm. That's right! Me, a good ole, midwestern farm girl. Animals. Animal shit. Cows. Minnesota. Corn. Rural-ness. Dirt. Hashtag FarmLyfe. That was my life. That was the life I knew.

Today, I don't regret being raised that way one bit. But man, oh man, when I was a kid, I *hated* living on a farm, especially a farm in Minnesota – talk about freezing!

I used to dream about living in a warm city. I imagined palm trees. I imagined the ocean breeze in my face, my hair blowing. I imagined civilization with actual people, not just farm animals. I imagined cute surfer dudes walking around everywhere.

Little did I know, when I was daydreaming as a child, I was asking The Universe for that experience. I was "attracting" that life. I just didn't know it back then.

After graduating high school in Minnesota, I went to college in sunny Santa Barbara and lived in a beach shack right next to the ocean. Everything I imagined as a kid happened. It became my reality.

What was I doing when I was daydreaming? I was asking The Universe. And that's step one: Just Ask The Universe!

Let's dive in as to why this step is important.

It begins with energy. Energy is real! There's even an equation for it: e = MC2. There's energy all around us; when we move, when we interact with other people, when we walk, when we exercise... all over! Just like physical movements, thoughts have energy.

As a fun exercise, I like to remind myself of energy by rubbing my palms together swiftly, and lightly separating them to feel the heat of that energy.

Thoughts transmit energy as you sit there, think, and daydream.

The Universe is made of that same energy. The energy in you is all around. When you ask The Universe for something (whether you do it consciously or unconsciously), you're a magnet attracting the energy of The Universe to a specific desire, experience, or thing. When I was day-dreaming as a child, I was attracting a lifestyle. I was attracting Santa Barbara into my life even though I didn't know the power of my own thoughts.

Whether you believe in Manifestation or not, you're manifesting every day just by thinking and imagining. We ask The Universe for things all the time. Just this morning, I opened a magazine and saw an ad for a new Louis Vuitton bag I want. I didn't do it consciously, but I imagined holding that bag. Well, I'm attracting it (but the bag would look mighty fine under my arm, not gonna lie).

I've also manifested shitty things, unintentionally of course. Just the other day, I was thinking about how bad I am with computers. By doing that, I'm putting out into The Universe how technology hates me. Well guess what? When I think about how shitty I am with technology, it all goes haywire. My internet connection gets lost. Pop ups appear out of nowhere. Emails get delayed. It sucks. But I'm human. You're human.

We all have negative thoughts from time to time. We ask The Universe for great things, and by thinking negative thoughts, we ask The Universe for awful things.

Step 1: Just Ask the Universe

Just know that manifestation starts with asking. Day-dreaming. Imagination. Or you can attract things by just asking The Universe out loud.

Manifesting Bitch Kit

Use the workbook sheet below. Sit down at home, like *right now...* close your eyes. Imagine that you're a giant magnet and say "Universe, I'm asking that you bring me (you fill in the blank)." Write it down in the workbook sheet. It can be anything. Something small, something big! Whatever! Continue reading this book and think about that desire and find out what more you need to do to manifest it into your life.

_____

_____

_____

_____

_____

_____

_____

_____

_____

Step 1: Just Ask the Universe

_____

_____

_____

_____

_____

_____

_____

_____

_____

_____

_____

_____

_____

_____

_____

_____

Chapter 2

STEP 2: FAKE IT 'TIL YOU MAKE IT!

So, you've asked The Universe for your desire. You've thought about it. You've written it down in your work-book sheet. Now it's time for the second step: Fake It 'til You Make It! What does that mean? Now what? Well, it's time for one of my favorite steps (who am I kidding? They're all my favorite steps!).

You must act as though your desire is already in your life. It's here! Yay! You have it! Celebrate, damnit!

As you grow from step 1 to 2, don't think. Imagine. Just imagine having that thing, having that designer bag, that dream vacation, or that dream job.

What does it feel like to drive that new car you want? What do you do at your new job that you're manifesting? Who are your coworkers? Are they friendly? Where do you work? An office? At home? What do you look like when you work? How do you feel entering your new apartment? How do you cook in your dream kitchen?

What are you cooking in your dream kitchen? What aspects fall in your life from having this specific desire? Imagine the answers to these questions.

Perhaps you just do step one by asking The Universe for your intended desire. That's fine. But if you want to consciously perfect this manifestation process, it's not enough to ask for what you want. Every step is just as important as the last. Much like the title of the chapter, you have to pretend like you already have what you want.

Asking is one thing, but what does it actually feel like to have your intended desire? When you *imagine* how your life would be, you raise your energetic vibration, attracting the "want" into your life even more. This, in turn, will bring up positive emotions so that you effectively perform step 2 of my manifestation process.

It seems weird, right? What kind of crazy person acts like they have something they don't? Well guess what, it's part of the manifestation process, and it's fun. Well, it should be. Think of this step as a little game!

This step should be light and fun (side note: no step should feel pushed or forced). When I first studied manifestation, I would push this step. I would focus so fucking hard. I would *think* instead of *imagine* (and there's a difference). Thinking implies forcefulness and heaviness, but *imagination* implies using your heart and emotions to picture your ideal life.

I specifically forced myself to think (and not imagine) when it came to love. I would force myself to think about having a boyfriend, and with all the cerebral thoughts, it wasn't fun or light anymore. It brought up past wounds I had from emotionally unstable relationships. In trying to manifest something I wanted, I actually brought back emotional trauma.

We don't want that. I had to take a step back. And if this happens to you, if you're pretending you have something and it's bringing back traumatic emotions, start over. Seriously. Go back to step one, and manifest something else. You're not ready for love if it's bringing up past wounds. And that's okay. Maybe you need to manifest self-love before you manifest love with someone else. Okay... my tangent is done.

As you have fun playing make believe (emphasis on the fun), what would it mean to have this desire you asked for? What emotions come up? Glee? Excitement? Relief? Peacefulness?

Step 2: Fake It 'Til You Make It!

We'll get to this later in the book, but there are different ways to imagine. You can literally just mediate, visualize, and play through what it's like to have the thing. You can use mantras, and you can literally have an out-loud conversation with yourself pretending like you have it.

Manifesting Bitch Kit

Step 2 should be part of your daily routine. But for this book, take that thing you asked for in step 1. Now imagine you have it. It's here! In the worksheet below, write down the emotions you feel during this imagination process. Peacefulness? Excitement? Harmony? Happiness? Glee? If they're not positive emotions, go back to step 1. Let these positive emotions fill your entire body and energy. Then write them down.

_____

_____

_____

_____

_____

_____

_____

_____

_____

_____

Step 2: Fake It 'Til You Make It!

_____

_____

_____

_____

_____

_____

_____

_____

_____

_____

_____

_____

_____

_____

_____

Chapter 3

STEP 3: RELEASE IT LIKE YOU JUST DON'T CARE!

So, you've asked The Universe for what you want. You've *imagined* it was part of your life. Now let go. Release It Like You Just Don't Care!

Don't overthink this step. Act like, "Huh... yeah... whatever."

When I was first learning about manifestation, I didn't understand this step. I wanted to manifest a better social life when I moved from Santa Barbara to Los Angeles. I was lonely. I barely had any friends or connections, and I was drowning in solitude.

I said to myself, "you manifest things all the time. Let's do it. I'm going to manifest a better social life."

I imagined going to fun parties and having friends and real connections. I unknowingly shifted from imagining and daydreaming to *obsessing* about it.

But then as I got busy with work, I just let the desire go. I even emailed myself an email saying, "I want a better social life." I deleted the email as work became too hectic. And guess what? As soon as I released (deleted the email) the desire, I made my first friend in Los Angeles while hiking Runyon Canyon. It was a hot Saturday. And that's where I met Haydee.

Releasing a desire is a lot harder than it seems. Obviously. When you care about something and want it so badly, it's easy to obsess instead of imagine. And I get it, I've been there. You wouldn't be reading this book if you *didn't* want something so badly in your life. But releasing the desire/want is just as important as the other steps. You have to do it. You have to let the desire go.

Why do we do this? It sounds odd, right? Most people think manifestation means thinking about your desire all day and all night! Well guess what, babe, that's how you lose sleep and stress out. That's how you go from imagining to obsessing and freaking out. And we don't want that. You'll go mad.

Here's why you release the desire into The Universe – first off, by focusing solely on your desire nonstop, you're building tension and anxiety and stress. Bad things. Eventually your focus goes from thinking about having something to, "why *don't* I have this? Why isn't my desire in my life yet?"

Releasing is about give and take. You need to give *up* your desire to The Universe and let The Universe do its part in this process. The Universe has work to do too! It's not all on you.

Imagine your desire is inside a bubble. Blow the bubble, let it grow, fill it up, then let that bubble fly away. Stop focusing, and trust that The Universe is already in the process of giving you what you want.

By releasing your desire, you're telling The Universe, "Yeah... dude. Yeah, Universe. I know I'll get my desire, so I shouldn't worry or lose sleep over it. The Universe will do its job. So whatevs."

But that's easier said than done, right? I know for me, this is a hard step because if I've been thinking about a desire, it encompasses all parts of me. But it's important to step back.

Releasing is just as important as the prior steps.

Manifesting Bitch Kit

Write down the desire you thought of in step 1. Rip this workbook sheet out and bury it in the ground. Never look at it again. And even though it's easier said than done, try not to dwell on it. Focus on other new desires and possible wants. Know that you did your part. You asked the universe for that promotion or that purse or whatever. You imagined having it, and now it's time for the Universe to do its part.

_____

_____

_____

_____

_____

_____

_____

_____

_____

_____

_____

_____

_____

_____

_____

_____

_____

_____

_____

_____

_____

_____

_____

_____

Chapter 4

STEP 4: INSPIRED ACTION

Now that you've done steps 1 through 3, it's time for step 4: Inspired action.

Before we move on, check in.

What's going on in your life? Anything? Nothing? Lots of things?

You might discover fun synchronicities popping up, or maybe you're viewing life from a different perspective – realizing that everything happening to you aligns with your thoughts.

Don't dwell on it but be grateful for those (if any) synchronicities that appear in your world.

Maybe you're trying to attract a brand-new Tesla into your life. I know I want one. You thought about driving a black Tesla. Then you released the desire into The Universe.

After steps 1 through 3, maybe you don't yet have a Tesla, but you're seeing black Tesla's showing up in your life everywhere – on your way to work, at your friend's house, all over!

Alright – Inspired Action is our second to last step in the manifestation process.

When you hear the word "action," it sounds like work, but this isn't work – at least not in the traditional sense.

Inspired Action means that you take the next actionable steps toward your desire based on signs from The Universe.

The Universe will send you messages of the next best actionable steps to take to obtain your desire via 3 main ways:

1. Physical Message/Meeting

2. Digital (Email/Social Media)

3. Intuitive Guidance

1. Physical Message/Meeting

Physical messages are my favorite. Maybe you see a physical sign that says "travel the world" along with a website about traveling the world. Maybe you meet a friend's dog, and the person who owns the dog tells you where they adopted that dog, and a fluffy, loving friend is just what you wanted.

If you get a physical message to take action, The Universe may bring someone into your life, and that person may ask something of you. Maybe your friend introduces you to a kickass man who makes you feel like yourself – a man that brings sparkles into your life (and bonus points if he's sexy as hell). Maybe this is The Universe introducing you to your soul mate! Take that man! The Universe is telling you to take action! Ask him out, damnit!

I remember just last year, I asked The Universe for a YSL bag... (sometimes I ask for materialistic things, but that's okay. Asking for abundance and fashion is okay. There's a reason you want those things, and it's all leading you to live your life's purpose – okay, rant over). Anywho, I asked The Universe for a Yves Saint Laurent bag. I'd browse websites and scroll through the YSL Instagram page. And I imagined having that bag, but the problem was that I didn't have a job that paid enough for a YSL bag. Now, full disclosure, I do not condone excessive gambling, but I went to Vegas, and all I brought with me was $50. I wasn't going to take out more than $50. I saw a YSL bag in the casino at the Flamingo, and I was like, "this is it. I gotta gamble in the Flamingo."

Now, listen – I never gamble. Like, I don't even know how to play craps or blackjack, but The Universe sent that physical YSL bag message in the Flamingo, and I just had to drop everything and gamble. I played roulette with $50 in the Flamingo and turned it into $2500. This is a true story. There's even a photo of me with this bag on my Instagram page. I remember my boyfriend (now fiancé) being so shocked that I did it. And I said, "The Universe sent me a message to gamble here, and I had to." I haven't gambled since though... lol.

2. Digital (Email/Social Media)

In the age of technology, The Universe sends messages through the lovely worldwide net! Not just physical. You could receive a message to take inspired action through email or social media or any other digital source.

Maybe you receive an email about a job opportunity, or you see something on social media that calls to you. Did you try to manifest a higher-paying job? Well, if an interview request shows up in your email inbox, then take the interview.

Or maybe you will get a message to take action through an introductory email. This recently happened to me. A producer introduced himself via email, and I saw this as a message from The Universe to take action, so instead of just saying "hi" back, I responded by telling him about a new screenplay I'm working on, and he asked to read it. So always pay attention.

People don't just email you out of the blue. The Universe is at work, and things are shifting. Things are happening behind the scenes that you don't necessarily know about or see. Read that again.

Things are happening behind the scenes that you don't necessarily know about or see.

It's all because you are creating this life in conjunction with The Universe. Its gears are moving! Trust that! Don't get frustrated if you don't see things right away.

There are other messages you might receive through the digital world: an email, a friend request from a person you haven't seen in years, an online article that pops up, an ad pop up... you never know. That's why you have to be hyper aware of all the messages The Universe sends to you throughout the day. Just a day! You never know. Stay present. Stay alert.

3. Intuitive Guidance

The 3rd way The Universe sends messages is through intuitive guidance.

Intuitive guidance is the most difficult of the 3 I've listed. Intuitive guidance comes from within rather than through external sources.

Maybe your intuition tells you that if you want to make more money, you should invest in property or into particular stock.

You know it's your intuition when everyone says something otherwise, but your soul is like "I gotta do this!"

Something to remember when receiving intuitive messages is to know the difference between ego and intuition.

We all hear various voices in our head every day. Your thoughts run wild in that noggin of yours – thoughts about people, things, experiences, meetings, and more.

Contradictory messages plague the mind all the time. Intuition comes from the heart and gut. Whereas, the ego is influenced by the physical world around us, society, and what other people think. Ego isn't necessarily bad, it's just not intuition. Your intuition comes from a higher space –

whether you believe in God, The Universe, many Gods, or just energy – intuition is easy flowing and effortless.

You can tell if a message is from the ego if your mind goes to a million questions. The ego will want to know how, why, what, where.... all of it. The ego changes its mind and lives in fear.

So, if you're trying to get a promotion at work, and you hear a message in your head to perform an extra research report, but then you immediately go to, "Why am I doing this extra research report? Will it really help me?" You worry about it – that's a huge red flag that it's coming from your ego and not your intuition.

In conclusion – in order to take the next actionable steps (Inspired Action) toward your desire, *pay attention! Pay attention to the messages The Universe is sending you!*

Manifesting Bitch Kit

Look out for any digital, physical, or intuitive messages to-day, and write down 3 different simple action steps you can take to get closer to manifesting that thing you desire.

_____

_____

_____

_____

_____

_____

_____

_____

_____

_____

_____

_____

_____

Step 4: Inspired Action

_____

_____

_____

_____

_____

_____

_____

_____

_____

_____

_____

_____

_____

_____

_____

Chapter 5

STEP 5: RECEIVE IT, DUDE!

Receive it, Dude! You did it! Well, you think you've done it all...

You've asked, you've faked it, you've released it, and you've taken inspired action. Now what? What's possibly left to do after all that? It is time to receive what you asked for through The Universe.

Here are the 3 ways to receive a manifested desire:

1. Recognize It

2. Allow the Universe to Support You

3. Show Gratitude

1. Recognize It

First, recognize it. Say you were trying to manifest a new apartment – you faked it and imagined having it, and someone reached out to you about applying.

Through inspired action, you applied. It's as easy as that. And then, you get the offer. Just acknowledge that you got something that you've been trying to manifest. *Recognize* that The Universe gifted you with the manifestation.

Or if you do not yet have the intended desire, acknowledge and recognize the synchronicities in your life that apply to what you asked The Universe for. If you asked for a boyfriend, recognize the potential suitors in your life – see it, recognize it. Or if you're trying to manifest a new job, *recognize* the interview request you're receiving, or the job openings that appear in your inbox.

2. Allow The Universe To Support You

After recognizing that The Universe has given you this desire (or is showing you synchronicities), *allow The Universe to support you.*

You can lean on The Universe. Maybe it scares you now that you have this new apartment you asked for. How will you keep up with rent? What if something breaks? What if there's a water leak? Stop! Seriously! Just stop! Surrender to those feelings for a moment, but then stop those negative thoughts!

Celebrate what's good. You've manifested the apartment you wanted. You have it. It's here, and The Universe is here to tell you that you did this.

And maybe you haven't been accepted for that dream apartment yet. Lean into The Universe.

Some things take longer to manifest than others, and that's all part of Universal timing. Trust that it will come. Trust that it will support you.

For example, I'll be honest here, I've been manifesting to sell a screenplay I've been working on for a few years, and I imagined pitching and selling the screenplay with the utmost glee. Though it hasn't happened yet, I know it will, and my goal has manifested in a different way. One of my close friends just sold his first feature length screenplay with a famous actor attached to the project, and it's happening. Instead of being jealous, I'm super excited for him, and I know his success is a sign of success that'll come for me. Through his experience, I'm allowing The Universe to support me in my journey.

3. Show Gratitude

Be grateful for the messages you've received. Or if The Universe has granted you with your intended desire, receive that and be grateful.

Let The Universe know you're grateful for everything it has given to you and everything you'll be given in the future.

Gratitude is important. By being grateful, you'll heighten your ability to continue manifesting your desires in the future.

Everything in The Universe is give and take. When you manifest and do the work, you give, and The Universe takes it in. And once you've done the steps, it's your turn to accept (take) and let The Universe give to you. Then the cycle happens again and again.

Manifesting Bitch Kit

Acknowledge that the Universe brought you your intended desire from the first step. Thank the Universe and continue on. In the workbook sheet, literally write "Thank you, Universe! Thank you for bringing this new friend into my life." If you haven't yet received the thing you want, write in the workbook sheet that you're thankful for the synchronicities and that you're ready to receive your desire.

_____

_____

_____

_____

_____

_____

_____

_____

_____

Step 5: Receive It, Dude!

Part 2

EASY MANIFESTATION TOOLS

So, we've gone over the 5 steps of manifestation. Great! Now it's time to raise your vibration. Why? Because when we raise our energetic vibration, The Universe will give us what we want more easily. And how can we do that? Through fun, easy manifestation tools. This is personally my favorite part of manifestation!

Tools aren't just for building physical things like houses. They're also for building manifestation powers!

There are 5 simple tools I like to use to manifest my desires... just to amp up the vibration and attract things easily. All of the tools I use apply to the 5 steps of manifestation. Here they are. Are you ready?

1. This Ain't Your Momma's Vision Board

2. Basic Witch-y Candles

3. Manifestation Visualization

4. Manifestation Mantras & Affirmations

5. Gratitude Practice

After reading part 2, you'll up your manifestation game. You'll no longer be a manifesting newbie. We're bringing you up with the top players of manifestation... not that it's a competition or anything, but hey, let's go deeper into how we can use fun tools to attract the things you want.

Chapter 6

THIS AIN'T YOUR MOMMA'S VISION BOARD

Not that my mom actually has a vision board. Honestly, she probably should make a vision board. But my vision boards are a little different than the typical, basic bitch vision boards. Have I said vision enough?

First off, if you're unfamiliar with what a vision board is, where have you been? Are you even alive? A vision board is a dedicated poster with images, art, and words that express what you want to bring into your life. Maybe you tape a photo of your dream house or a photo of a healthy body to help manifest a fit life.

But the typical vision board can be basic. Like super basic. As basic as the latte I had this morning.

I used to just cut out things I wanted from Vogue magazines to put on my vision board. I'd think it'd be nice to have a certain designer dress, a hot boyfriend... but what I didn't realize is that those cutouts didn't bring up any emotion for me. They were just like, "eh, I want it, so let's put it on the vision board."

There are 3 easy steps for creating a more effective vision board that works!

Before even buying the cardboard for your vision board, meditate for a moment.

Think – first about the things you want in the broad sense: the dream job, the dream house, the dream life.

Then get more specific: a new Tesla, a new Mac laptop, a friend, a date. Then pay attention to the feelings and emotions that come up. Effortless and easy – always remember that.

Now go get a shit ton of magazines, cardboard, glue, and maybe even grab a few friends to do vision boards together – a vision board party!

Here are the 3 things you need in order to create a more effective vision board:

1. Emotional Images

2. Emotional Words

3. It's all about the Space

1. Emotional Images

The first step is to find *Emotional Images.*

Don't just grab images of things you want, but look through a magazine or the internet, and cut out the ones that bring up positive feelings from the heart and gut.

Do the images bring up the same emotions you felt when you imagined having that dream life? When you "Fake It 'til You Make it!" (Step 2 from Part 1), did these feelings come up? Did the image of a plant-filled apartment make you giddy and comfortable like when you imagined living in that dream home?

If you see a photo of a Costa Rican vacation, and it brings you the emotion of pure joy or adventure, then use it. If you see an image of a beautiful wedding gown, and it makes you tear up, use it! That's a sign that you really want it, and your emotion is amping up the energetic vibration! Glue or tape to your cork board/poster board and get going on that vision board.

2. Emotional Words

Now that you have *Emotional Images* for your vision board, it's time to find *Emotional Words* that you associate feeling with.

42

What words bring you a sense of purpose or motivation? For me, that's "hope!" Hope has been my go-to word for a few years now. It makes me feel positive and reassures me that I can have anything with hope. Hope makes me feel safe.

Don't just pick a word because it feels "cool" or interesting. Find words that fill you with inspiration, wonder, and all-encompassing positive emotions.

Now write it in a way that enhances your feeling *or* if you're super handy, maybe write it with letters using PowerPoint or Photoshop, or whatever really enhances the way you feel about the word.

Side note; you'll want to be able to see your vision board daily, so make sure when you tape up the images and words, you do so in a way that makes you happy, whether that means keeping it organized and beautiful, or asymmetrical and fun.

3. It's All About The Space

Now that you've taped/glued on *Emotional Images* and *Emotional Words*, find a sacred space for your vision board. Let it be the first and last thing you see every day to remind you of what you want to manifest into your life.

I keep mine in my writing room (I could call this space an office, but the word "office" doesn't make me feel very positive, so I call it my writing room).

Look at that vision board, and if it loses its vibration, if you're not feeling as excited to see it every day, make a new board. No one says you have to use *one* vision board for your whole life.

Manifesting Bitch Kit

3 Month Vision Board Challenge!

Using the workbook sheet below, write the various things you'd like. Now get magazines and cardboard and create your vision board. Now let's do the 3-month vision board challenge. Create a vision board. After 3 months, take off the images and words that resonate with you and create a new vision board for the next 3 months.

In your workbook, write down any clues towards what you want. Did you get the bag you taped on your board? Did you save that extra 5k you wanted? Look around for the synchronicities. And if you didn't manifest one of the images/words, and that desire still resonates with you, tape it to your new vision board. Keep it close to your bed, so you see it when you wake up and when you fall asleep.

_____

_____

_____

_____

_____

Manifest it, Bitch

_____

_____

_____

_____

_____

_____

_____

_____

_____

_____

_____

_____

_____

_____

Chapter 7

BASIC WITCH-Y CANDLES

As a Los Angeleno basic witch, I can't write a manifestation book without mentioning intention candles! First off, intention candles are just that – candles used to help you set and attain an intention.

Intention candles are so fun. I love fire. It's my favorite element to play with.

I discovered the power of intention candles in college. I was dating a terrible, emotionally abusive man, but I convinced myself he was perfect for me. I thought I could help our love by lighting a love intention candle. I was open to The Universe, said "bring me the best loving partnership," and a few months later, I met my current soulmate and FIANCÉ! That's right! The emotionally abusive relationship ended, and a new, perfect one began.

Consider going to your local new age shop, find a specific colored candle, and go for it. Ask for the 4-day candles! They're a little thicker, and make sure to get a glass holder. I use yellow for luck and creativity, green for money, red for relationship, and white and purple for enhanced spirituality.

These are basic colors, and you can get even deeper into it, like using multi-colored candles or whatever, but this is a good place to start. Some magic/new age shops will even make you a custom candle. Just make sure you give the practitioner as many details as possible about what you want.

Now that you have the candle, meditate with it. Think about what it is you want. Just like steps 1 through 3 – ask, fake it, then release it into the candle. Some people get so caught up in what colors they should use, but all in all, the *most important* step to take when using intention candles is to meditate with the candle and set the intention.

Then you can carve fun symbols. I like to carve my name, the thing I want, my astrological sign, and some other symbols that just come to me. When I want money, I carve a specific amount onto the candle. If you want to get real fancy, you can look up specific runes and such online or at your local book shop.

I also like to anoint the candle with various oils you can get from new age shops. I ask for good luck oil, and they usually have a ton of options. And if you want, add glitter! I try to keep this book nondenominational, but it is said that the flame can be seen all along the astral plane, and adding glitter enhances its visibility!

Now it's time to light that candle. I use a saucepan and place it in the kitchen sink. Fill it with water, then put the candle inside. Keep the candle in a safe space such as the sink or if you don't have any pets, a bathtub.

The key is to keep the candle lit until it is completely out! Never blow out the candle! If you need to put out the flame for safety reasons, you can snuff it out with a snuffer (you can usually buy one at a new age shop) or by eliminating the oxygen in the flame. To do that, you can place a ceramic mug over the candle until the flame goes out. Just make sure to light the candle again as soon as you can! Keep the intention alive!

As you pass the lit candle, think about the intention without attachment to a particular outcome. "Fake It 'til You Make It" (Step 2 of Part 1) as you pass the candle. Let the flame burn out. When the flame is out, throw/recycle the glass! "Release It Like You Just Don't Care" (Step 3 of Part 1).

Release the intention and don't obsess over it. It's The Universe's time to bring the intention to you. Just like our

5-step process. When you create and light a magic intention candle, you must follow the same manifestation steps laid out in Part 1. So, get rid of the glass. Some people also like to bury the glass.

You might say, "but Mary, what if the candle flame goes out on its own? What if it doesn't burn all the way down?" Here's the good news – you can still manifest what you want, but maybe you need to restructure the intention and redo the candle.

When the flame doesn't go according to plan, it's a sign that you need to start the intention candle again. Start all over. Get rid of the old candle and begin again.

Restructure the intention candle coming from your highest vibrational energy.

Conclusion: The Intention candle is all about what you put into it. The colors, oil, symbols all enhance its powers, but at the end of the day, you have to put in the work and meditate with the candle. The power of the intention is in you.

Manifesting Bitch Kit

Think about that first desire you had in mind in Chapter 1 – Just Ask The Universe. Does it have to do with love, money, career, life purpose? Find a single-color candle. I like to go to new age shops, but you can even go to a typical store – just try to stay away from scented candles.

Hold the candle, think about what you want, anoint it and carve it if you would like, and when you're ready, light it. Keep it lit until it's out if you can. Remember to keep it in a water-filled saucepan in the sink or a cauldron if you have one. Then, when the candle flame is out, get rid of the glass. Use the worksheet book below to record what colored candle you purchased and what it is you want.

_____

_____

_____

_____

_____

_____

_____

_____

_____

_____

_____

_____

_____

_____

_____

_____

_____

_____

_____

_____

_____

_____

_____

Chapter 8

MANIFESTATION VISUALIZATION

Every morning, before I go on Instagram or check my ever-growing inbox, I sit up, close my eyes, center myself, and then think of *one* thing I would like to attract into my life.

I think about that one desire for just two minutes every morning. I imagine myself in a bubble having this one thing. I think about what it would feel like... aka I "Fake It 'til I Make It" - Step 2 from Part 1. I continue watching myself in that bubble. I imagine how happy I am with this thing.

This morning, I visualized my ideal house. Like super ideal, even better than Barbie's Malibu house. I imagined the modern kitchen, open floor plan. I imagined opening the front door, swimming in the pool in the backyard, and then I pictured myself with my fiancé enjoying this sacred space. I visualized my desire in a little bubble. Then, I released the desire and let that bubble float away up into The Universe.

This is a simple manifestation visualization practice, and it's super easy because you don't need to buy anything, and you don't need to prepare anything. You just need your mind and a quiet place.

Here are some steps for a typical manifestation visualization:

1. Get Centered

2. Think About One Thing

3. Imagination, Baby!

1. Get Centered

Get centered before you do anything else! Seriously! Most of us turn on our phones as soon as we wake up. Sometimes I still do, but no. Don't be tempted.

Just quiet your mind. Start the day off right. To get centered, wake up and focus on your breathing and cut off the shit or busy thoughts! You can focus on your breath to help cut the mind noise.

Breathe in for 4 seconds, hold your breath for 4 seconds, then exhale for 4 seconds. Repeat until you are *really* in the zone and centered. You'll know you're centered when the inner-voice chatter disappears.

Another way to cut out the bullshit thoughts and get centered is to focus on the back of your eyelids.

Why do we do this? Well, the point of getting centered is to A: Keep you calm and content. B: raise your vibrational energy and C: To keep you open and ready to receive.

2. Think About One Thing

Now that you're centered, it's time to think about one thing you want. Explore the power of your mind and visualization practice. Pick that one thing. Maybe this morning you decide to visualize yourself on vacation in the Mediterranean. Choose it. Accept it. Just that one thing. You can visualize something else tomorrow, but for today, think about a luxurious Mediterranean vacation.

3. Imagination, Baby!

Focus on what it would be like to have that one thing.

Imagine getting off the plane in Greece. Imagine the sand beneath your feet. How does it feel? Is there a breeze?

Imagine the food. What's the texture of the food? Get really deep into this visualization practice. What is it like to be in the Mediterranean? Just imagine it for as long as it feels good. That could be 2 minutes, it could be 10 minutes, but when you're ready, realize it.

Once you've completed the visualization step, release the intention – step 3 of the manifestation process per Part 1: "Release It Like You Just Don't Care." Go back to your body. Breathe. Relax. Smile. Focus on your breath and the back of your eyelids.

This visualization practice works! It really does. When you start your morning this way, you're raising your vibration, aligning yourself with The Universe.

A bonus effect is that you feel good for the rest of the day. Trust me. It is way better to start your day off by thinking about a vacation in Greece than it is to check work emails on your phone. You can check those emails when you're at work, okay.

Manifesting Bitch Kit

Using the workbook sheet below, I want you to write down the one thing you're going to visualize *before* you do a morning visualization process. It will help get you focused. Then once you're ready, go ahead and try it. Do the 3 steps of visualization. Get centered, think about that one thing and imagine.

_____

_____

_____

_____

_____

_____

_____

_____

_____

_____

_____

_____

_____

_____

_____

_____

_____

_____

_____

_____

_____

_____

_____

_____

_____

_____

Chapter 9

MANIFESTATION MANTRAS AND AFFIRMATIONS

Mantras! Mantras! Mantras! It's all about the mantras! If manifestation visualization is difficult for you, try instead closing your eyes and chanting mantras and affirmations either aloud or in your head.

What are mantras? Mantras are a group of words sacred to *you* that aid in obtaining your goals and higher self. You can find helpful mantras online, from gurus, or just write them on your own.

I was recently unemployed not so long ago. I was applying for jobs left and right. I'd go on interviews and pass along more and more resumes, but I wasn't getting any job offers. Though the experience felt negative, I tried to stay positive. I could've stayed up all night in stress. Instead, I would chant, "the perfect job for the perfect pay is on its way." Before I let myself get stressed about the job hunt, I'd continue the mantra: "the perfect job for the perfect pay is on its way." The mantra is fun. It rhymes, and it keeps you open to the possibilities. If you're in a similar situation, take it. It's yours. Use it whenever you want as much as you want!

I also like, "money flows easily and effortlessly to me." Mantras are great when you're one of those people who can't just sit down and meditate. It keeps you focused and thinking about the mantra raises the vibration of your thoughts, so that they come to fruition.

Repeat the mantra for 2 minutes a day. We'll call it the 2 for 2 mantra challenge. Every day for two weeks, dedicate 2 minutes to a new mantra every day. That's right. Switch it up. Look online for a fun mantra or create a new one each time you chant. You can say aloud or to yourself.

Just like mantras, affirmations assist with the manifestation process.

While mantras tend to be about outwardly matters, affirmations are in the first position.

Affirmations can help negate negative thoughts and feelings. If you're feeling negative about your self-confidence, you might want to use an affirmation such as: "I am beautiful. I am radiant. I am magical!" As with mantras, you can find many affirmations online, from gurus, or write them yourself.

Why this works; mantras and affirmations raise your vibration, bring about positive emotions, and solidify the desire in motion. And it's easy because you can do it anywhere. You can use mantras and affirmations any part of the day. You can start your morning off saying them in the shower. You can say them at work... maybe in your head because you might sound like a crazy person at the office chanting things, but you know what, go for it if you would like to.

Manifesting Bitch Kit

Use the workbook sheet to create and write down the mantras you'll use for the 2 for 2 mantra challenge. Try to split them up by different life areas. You could have a mantra for manifesting something with spirituality, money and abundance, love, and health.

_____

_____

_____

_____

_____

_____

_____

_____

_____

_____

_____

_____

_____

_____

_____

_____

_____

_____

_____

_____

_____

_____

_____

_____

_____

_____

Chapter 10

GRATITUDE PRACTICE

Not gonna lie, I love this tool, but I love every manifestation tool... what can I say?

Gratitude practice is a tool you can use even if you don't have certain things you want.

My gratitude practice is telling The Universe you're grateful for something, even though you don't have it. And The Universe responds to it like a magnet. The Universe loves gratitude, and you might not know it, but you do too! It is an instant way to bring positivity into your life.

First off, list down everything you're grateful for. Start simple; "I'm grateful for this new day, I'm grateful for a bed, I'm grateful for my apartment/house...", and really be grateful for the things you have. Seriously. Be grateful for the water you use to clean your face and brush your teeth. Be grateful for a roof over your head. Be grateful for the people in your life. Because guess what? No matter where you are in life, there is something to be grateful for. Truly.

Before moving onto the next step, be grateful and live in it. Smile. Breathe it. Feel it.

Then it gets more fun! List things you're grateful for that you don't yet have, but you want. Use that same positivity you have for the things you are grateful for and apply it to the things you don't have. I'm grateful for my Tesla (that's what I'm manifesting right now), I'm grateful for my amazing beach house.

Having a solid gratitude practice works! I mean, all the tools work, but gratitude is just another practice to raise your vibration and make it easier for you to manifest anything. In addition, being grateful is proven to boost your mood. Just a nice side effect to the work you're already doing.

Manifesting Bitch Kit

List the things you're grateful for. Start simple. Then have fun and list the things you're grateful for that you don't yet have but would like to attract into your life.

_____

_____

_____

_____

_____

_____

_____

_____

_____

_____

_____

_____

Gratitude Practice

_____

_____

_____

_____

_____

_____

_____

_____

_____

_____

_____

_____

_____

_____

_____

_____

Part 3

MANIFESTATION IN EVERYDAY LIFE

You've learned the 5 steps of manifestation. Just ask The Universe, Fake It 'til You Make It, Release It Like You Just Don't Care, Inspired Action, and Receive It, Dude.

You've learned the tools to up your manifestation game and raise your vibration. But, let's get real – real world real, right? How can you manifest modern-world, everyday things? How can we use the tools we've already learned to get everyday things?

It's like... one thing to know the steps and be like a super cool, hippie, spiritual Goddess, but that can't help you with real-life things.

When it comes to manifestation and all things desire, most of us all want the same things: money, love, and experience. Because for you, that's what life's all about.

You're meant to live a happy life. You're meant to go on adventures. You're meant to experience love. You're meant to live out your life's purpose and just have nice shit, and there are reasons you have the desires you do, and it's all because The Universe wants what's best for you. The Universe wants you to live your best life.

Part 3 is about manifestation in everyday life. You'll take what we've learned and apply it to manifest those things we all want. Let's manifest money, love, and experiences through the tools we've already discussed and using the 5 basic steps.

So... are you ready to manifest money, love, and adventures? Of course you are. Let's go.

I've broken Part 3 into chapters, and I won't be offended if you skip one, but at some point, you're gonna want to manifest all these things:

1.   More Moola, Please!

2.   I want Love, Baby!

3.   Manifesting Experience

Chapter 11

MORE MOOLA, PLEASE!

Money is a form of energy just like anything else. So, let's start from square one. Before continuing on to money manifestation, reframe your perception of money. You need to have a healthy relationship with it, just like having healthy relationships with friends and loved ones. It's important to have a functional relationship with abundance, AKA money. And first off, think of money as abundance.

Instead of picturing that dollar sign, the perceived notion of bills and payday, think of this source as *abundance*. Get used to saying that word and get used to using it in everyday life.

In my own life, it took me a while to realize that money isn't just about things. It's not just about having designer clothes or going on luxurious vacations with fruity cocktails. I mean, yeah, money is about that too, and those things are nice and all, but money, or *abundance*, for me, is about freedom. It's about security. It's about lifting worry and stress.

Like, can you believe? Abundance is a form of energy we use to get the things we need and want. Money is not the douchey boyfriend you think it is (side note; In fact, I think abundance is female, and even giving money a gender can help shape your perception).

Money (*abundance*) isn't there to haunt your dreams and stress you out. Abundance is good. It should be good. You just have to change your mindset about it before you try to manifest it.

Whether you know your life purpose/career goals or not, just know that money (abundance) is a necessary energy exchange in the grand scheme of your existence.

Now that we're clearer on the type of relationship you must have with abundance, let's move onto actually manifesting it, yes?

I've broken down each of these manifestation applications based on your career/money making situation.

1.   You Don't Know Your Life Purpose

2.   You Know Your Life Purpose/Career Goals, But It's Not Happening

3.   You Just Want Money

1. You Don't Know Your Life Purpose

If you don't know your life purpose/career destiny, manifesting your life purpose is the ultimate objective.

First, accept that it's okay not to know. That's great. You're open to what The Universe will show you.

Using all the previous steps, imagine a life where you're happy and abundant. That's all you need to do. Why, you ask? Because if you imagine yourself happy in your career, you'll attract a job that you'll actually enjoy!

You don't want to manifest a career just to have a career. And when you're happy, it's easier to manifest more and more.

What kind of life do you want to live? What would work look like for you? Do you have coworkers? Do you work from home? Do you want a luxurious office? How would you spend your money? What would your schedule be like? Would you have an impact? Recognition? New opportunities will arise – then through inspired action from Part 1, you'll continue on.

The truth of the matter is that most people don't know what their life purpose is, and the world puts so much pressure on all of us to know from childhood what we want to do with our lives.

I was working with a manifestation client who struggled with what she wanted. It stressed her out. Her friends all knew what they wanted to do with their lives, but the harder she tried to figure it all out, the more stress and anxiety bubbled up. Then I asked her who she was jealous of. And by jealous, I mean jealous in a good way. I asked her out of all the people she follows on Instagram, whose page is like, "damn, I wish I could live like that."

I know we all show the world the best version of ourselves on Insta, but sometimes it can be a nice tool to look at when you're trying to figure out what your life purpose is.

She felt jealous of a fitness instructor she followed on Instagram. She would see the fitness instructor post about helping people get fit, and see her live this healthy lifestyle, and she manifested a message about her own life purpose. She signed up to take yoga teacher training the next day, and after completing her training and teaching for 1 year, she hasn't looked back!

2. You Know Your Life Purpose/Career Goals, But It's Not Happening

This is one I struggle with all the time. I think most people in this boat forget Step 3 from Part 1: "Release It Like You Just Don't Care."

You struggle with attaining your career goals, and you dwell all the time. Sometimes I *obsess* about my career desires.

You may think and think about how badly you want it until it stresses you out. People with this issue also tend to think about the situation they're already in instead of pretending like they're already doing what they know they want to do. They dwell on what's going wrong in their life. They dwell on how they're stuck – how everyone else has "made it," but they have not.

If you *know* what you want, and you *know* your life purpose, but it's not just happening, first off – be positive. *Be grateful for the life you have.*

Use the manifestation tools in this book, especially the gratitude practice, but realize that everything will happen in perfect timing. Trust that your manifestation process works, and some things take a long time to manifest. The right time is different for everyone. The right time for you is different than the right time for me. That's okay. That's beautiful.

Some desires take a day to manifest, some desires take months, years, but you must trust. I know that's easier said than done but keep actively using a gratitude practice every damn day! Start your morning with a visualization.

Know that right now, at this very moment, you *are* living your best life. We're all living our best life. Somewhere in The Universe, you already have that thing you want. Your responsibility is to live life effortlessly and continue to live your best life with or without your desire. Just know that even if you don't have it in the physical world/realm, it will happen. It is happening somewhere out there. Call it a celestial plane, another dimension, or just a theory, but you have the desire. It's just not in *your* reality... *yet.*

3. You Just Want Money

Maybe you don't want to work or make a statement in your career, which is awesome. Many millionaires in the world put in much less effort than anyone else. Passive income. Investments. All of it.

In order to attract *abundance* into your life without a career objective, think about what money will mean for you. Freedom, peace, security? Feel those emotions.

Use certain tools like candles from Part 2 and visualization. Live like a millionaire. Millionaires are smart with their money. They invest, spend wisely, and don't make stupid purchases.

Who knows? Maybe you'll get a random inheritance? Or you'll be inspired to invest a small amount of money into a stock. Maybe a surprise tax refund will show up in the mail. You never know. Be open to what The Universe may bring you.

Every single day, it's important to think like you have money and abundance, talk positively about money, and have a healthy relationship with money (abundance). Most people have a weird, unhealthy, passive-aggressive relationship with wealth. But this relationship is just as important as personal ones! Truly!

Manifesting Bitch Kit

Monthly money Monday shopping spree; this is a fun one.

The only rule is that you can't use it to buy a gift for someone. Using your workbook sheet below, every Monday, make a list of all the things you'd buy with an extra $1000, and go up to $2000 the following Monday, then $3000 until the month is over. You can list anything. For example, on the first Monday, if I had an extra $1000, I would buy a facial, a dress from Bloomingdales, extra magic candles (of course), a trip to Disneyland, and a massage... Then go up to $2000 the following Monday, and list what you would spend it on. That's it! And really imagine that you are going to buy these things.

_____

_____

_____

_____

_____

_____

Manifest it, Bitch

_____

_____

_____

_____

_____

_____

_____

_____

_____

_____

_____

_____

_____

_____

_____

Chapter 12

I WANT LOVE, BABY!

Now onto something you cannot buy – love! Love is, in my opinion, the best part of life: love between friends, love between soulmates, love between family, and love with self.

Love is the closest we can get to a higher power/God/The Universe/whatever you choose to believe in.

I've broken down each of these manifestation applications based on your love situation:

1. You Want a Soulmate

2. You're in a Relationship, but You want to Ignite the Spark

3. Attracting Sex & Spice & Everything Nice

1. You Want A Soulmate

You're single, and you want to find your soulmate, some-one you can spend the rest of your life with.

My friend – we'll call her Brook – had a similar situation. She was single all throughout college, and she kept at-tracting guys who just wanted to hook up with her – no strings attached-type situations. I gave her a red candle, told her to carve her initials and "soulmate" into the can-dle. I had her light the candle, and practice manifestation visualization from Part 2 every day next to the candle until it burned all the way through.

She started meeting more mature guys. I told her to write their names down, and the emotion associated with each of them. Then I asked her to write down words associated with her ideal soulmate. She wrote best friend. And next to one of the guys she met, she wrote "best friend." It was a match! And five years later, they got married in Ojai, CA, and they have a great life! When attracting a soulmate, it's best to know what words and emotions you associate your ideal soulmate with.

No b.s. now. Really think, how do you want to feel next to that person every day? Get *very* specific. The more you know what you want in a soulmate, the easier it'll be to attract one. If you're going to be with a significant other for life, what kind of person do you want to be with? How do you want to feel with that person when you wake up next to him or her in bed?

So, what is this story all about? Well A: you never know who your soulmate actually is until you know what it is you want.

And B: To know what you want, you have to identify the type of relationship that is necessary for you.

When attracting a soulmate, it's vital to know what and who your ideal soulmate is to you. Is he or she a best friend? Someone who will put you first? Is he or she someone that excites you?

Erase all the potential mates in your life. Forget about Joe from Tinder. Forget about that ex you're thinking about texting. Erase all images of past mates. Be open. When attracting a soulmate, it can be easy to think of a specific person in your life, but maybe that person isn't someone who can be your lifelong partner.

Once you've identified what kind of soulmate you want, use the 5 steps of manifestation from Part 1, and consider using a fun tool. I love to use intention candles for love along with a visualization practice as the candle burns. I suggest you start there.

In conclusion: Know what it is you want.

2. You're In A Relationship, But You Want To Ignite The Spark

You are in a relationship – one that you love – but you could do something more to ignite the spark. How can you improve the love you already have?

My boyfriend (now fiancé) is my soulmate, but last year was hard. We were both working very long hours, and when we got home, all we wanted to do was watch some TV and pass out, no date nights, even on Saturday's.

For us, I know vacations always ignite our spark. I used a vision board from Part 2 to attract a couple's trip. The next week, we took a weekend getaway trip to Palm Springs! It was just what we needed. He planned it all and surprised me. I was legitimately surprised, and we need to remember that little things and events like that are important for our relationship.

So, what can you do if you are in a relationship, but the spark is starting to die out? Well, what was it that attracted you to your partner in the first place? Identify the qualities you love about him or her and recognize the emotions that come up for you when you think about those qualities. Is your partner a great cook? Does your partner make you laugh? You can use a vision board or just a simple visualization of those qualities you love about your partner.

You can also have a straight-up conversation with your partner – by saying out loud what you want, you're *asking* (step 1 from Part 1) not only your partner, but The Universe. Ask for what you want. "Babe, I want adventurous sex," or "babe, I want romantic date nights every week."

3. Attracting Sex & Spice & Everything Nice

Maybe you're less inclined to go for the soulmate or improving love. Maybe you just want to attract sex and spice and everything nice, and that's awesome! Maybe things have gone stale, or dry (no pun intended). Spicing it up, attracting intimacy, and a spicier love life is the goal for you. Maybe you're with someone, or even if you just want to have more sex in a non-monogamous way, these tips can help you.

My friend – we'll call her Lisa – moved to LA after college, and her sexual life was nothing like college. She's a straight woman, and you'd think there'd be great men to have sex with in LA, but it was hard for her.

But think about it, in college, it's easy to manifest great sex because you're around so many young people, and you can seriously go to a party and visualize having a great sexual experience with one of the suitors. But after college, she was having difficulties.

One of the tools I didn't mention in the candle section, that I told her about, is a penis candle. And here's a tip, it's super fun to bring your girlfriends to your nearest new age shop to shop for these penis candles. I told her to write specifically her initials and great sex. I had her light the candle (candle magic from part 2) and visualize (visualization from part 2) an amazing sex life every day for about 5 minutes until the candle burned completely out. Then I told her to recycle the glass she used to burn the candle in and release the intention (step 3 from part 1). Lisa ended up meeting someone at a Farmer's Market, actually. They hooked up that afternoon, and although she wasn't looking for anything serious, they've now been dating for a year.

Manifesting Bitch Kit

I want you to be specific with what it is you want. Write it down in the workbook sheet below. If you want a soulmate, write down exactly what you want in a soulmate. If you want companionship, happiness, all of it – write it down. If you're trying to ignite the spark, what is it you want from your partner? Date nights? Vacations? And if you want sex, what kind of sex do you want? Adventurous? Passionate? Write it down below.

Then step 2 in the toolkit: pick a tool from part 2 that you want to use. Just pick one for now. Do you want to use visualization? A candle? A mantra? Gratitude? Use that one tool and have fun.

_____

_____

_____

_____

_____

_____

Manifest it, Bitch

_____

_____

_____

_____

_____

_____

_____

_____

_____

_____

_____

_____

_____

_____

_____

Chapter 13

MANIFESTING LIFE EXPERIENCES

Life is all about experience, right? That's why you're on this earth. You're here to travel, make friends, and enjoy this existence. In Chapter 13, I'll break down how you can manifest various life experiences into your life. I break it up into 3 sections:

1. Traveling the World

2. You want a Better Social Life

3. Bring Me Excitement!

1. Traveling The World

Traveling is an important life experience. It's a great way to see other places, cultures, and it gives you a sense of what it means to live on this planet. If you want to manifest travel, here are some tips:

Vision boards are great for this! And quite frankly, my favorite! It's easy to manifest travel using a vision board because you can actually see those places using photos. I love to post pictures on my vision boards of places that make me feel in awe of the world – places I'd love to see, places where I feel like I'm there from just a photo!

And just because you're not in Bora Bora now, doesn't mean you can't try to stir up the feeling that you are. You could go to the beach near your home and feel the sand in your feet. It's not exactly Bora Bora, but it's closer to Bora Bora than the hard wood floors in your apartment.

I recently manifested a beach vacation to Mexico, and all I did was look up Mexico vacations online. I went to a travel agent website and had fun with it. I didn't come from a place of like "Oh man... this will never happen." I looked up the vacations and pretended like, "oh, well I'd like to stay there and there and do this and that." Oh fun!

Manifesting Bitch Kit

Go online and look up various vacation spots you'd like to visit. Land on one and start planning online like you're really going to go there. Then write down in the workbook sheet below what you would do at the vacation spot. Maybe you want to go to Mexico like me. Write down that you're planning to swim with dolphins, go to the Mayan ruins, sip pina coladas – whatever!

_____

_____

_____

_____

_____

_____

_____

_____

_____

_____

Manifest it, Bitch

_____

_____

_____

_____

_____

_____

_____

_____

_____

_____

_____

_____

_____

_____

_____

_____

2. You Want A Better Social Life

Part of this great existence is that we're in it together. If you don't have friends to enjoy this life with, that can be hard. In this section, I'll give advice on how to manifest a better social life.

To manifest a better social life, first think about what kind of friends you want. Do you want friends who like to go out? Do you want friends who enjoy hiking and working out? Maybe you want friends who go to the beach or friends that give you amazing advice. Maybe you want to have financially secure and stable friends. Think about it.

Now that you've identified the type of friends you would like, use a tool from Part 2 to attract your ideal social life.

One of my favorite ways to manifest a better social life is to use the gratitude practice from Part 2. Pretend like you already have these friends and list what you're grateful for. Start a list. I'm grateful for weekly brunches with my friends. Or you could say you're grateful for weekly hikes with your friends. Maybe you're grateful to have support- ive friends that are there for you no matter what – friends that visit you in the hospital or support you when you're down.

Manifesting Bitch Kit

In your workbook sheet below, write that you're grateful for the social life you're trying to manifest.

_____

_____

_____

_____

_____

_____

_____

_____

_____

_____

_____

_____

Manifesting Life Experiences

3. Bring Me Excitement!

Life can get dull. We all know that. You get busy, tired, and stuck in the same routine.

Fortunately, we have manifestation to help us get out of any rut! Here are some tips for attracting excitement into your life.

I often get into quarterly ruts throughout the year – where I think, "wow, same old, same old." But I suggest using visualization from part 2 to manifest excitement.

Think about a moment in your life where you were truly elated. Maybe it was your wedding day or when you were on vacation. Maybe you felt elated after getting a promotion. Embrace that same elatedness. Feel it. Put your hand to your heart and feel it flutter as you bring up emotions of pure happiness and excitement.

You don't even have to know what it is that you specifically want. Just visualize yourself happy and feel that elatedness to the fullest. The more elated and excited you become, the more The Universe will bring you experiences that give you this feeling again and again.

Manifesting Bitch Kit

Using the workbook sheet below, write down various times in your life when you felt absolutely elated and excited! Writing it down will help you absorb the feeling easily. This, in turn, will help you to visualize and manifest excitement into your life.

_____

_____

_____

_____

_____

_____

_____

_____

_____

_____

_____

_____

_____

_____

_____

_____

_____

_____

_____

_____

_____

_____

_____

_____

_____

_____

Part 4

WHAT TO DO WHEN THE PROCESSES AREN'T WORKING

You've gone through the steps. You've used the tools. You took my advice and actively used the workbook sheets.

But maybe you're like, "Mary, this shit ain't working. I'm feeling fucking negative, and everything you told me to do... I'm doing it, and I still don't have a Versace dress."

Okay, I get it. That's what this part is for.

It's easy to stay at this pity party. Believe me – I've been there. I still get to that point, but then I remember that The Universe is on my side. And I use steps to help me get out of this negative space.

It's all part of this manifestation game we're all living. When the processes aren't working, use the following chapters:

1. Detach from the Outcome

2. Releasing the Negative Manifestation

3. Redo

Chapter 14

DETACH FROM THE OUTCOME

So, you feel like it's not working. You've done all the steps. You think you're in a high vibrational space ready to visualize and receive, but nothing. Nada. Nope.

You're not alone. The first step is to detach from the outcome. Here's how you do that:

1. Recognize the Negative Experience

2. Accept the Negative Experience as a Lesson

3. Surrender

1. Recognize The Negative Experience

Acknowledge that you didn't get what you wanted. Recognize that your desire hasn't become part of your reality... *yet.*

Avoid calling the experience bad. Just say, "that was not very positive for me. It was a little shitty, but things will get better."

That's the first step to detach from the outcome.

2. Accept The Negative Experience As A Lesson

You've had this negative experience trying to manifest something, but it didn't come to fruition.

Ask yourself what this experience was trying to teach you. Ask The Universe why it happened.

Why did you manifest a not-so-positive experience that didn't raise your vibration?

Listen to your intuition. Sometimes it's not so obvious. When I first experimented with manifestation, my biggest problem was trying to release the intention (from step 3 of Part 1). I'm still working on this step. I often feel so attached to the outcome, that manifestation doesn't feel fun and playful. I get back to that time when I was in high school striving for perfect grades and test scores. Pushing and pushing... and then nothing but negative emotions. And that's no good.

I am not a spirit guide, Goddess, or anything of the like. I'm human. You're human. We're all human. But do take responsibility for the negative thoughts/experiences you have. Accept that we all have negative thoughts. Even the most spiritual people on the planet aren't positive 100% of the time. The Universe works in waves much like the stock market.

Sometimes your vibration is extremely high, and sometimes you're like, "why am I manifesting all this shit? Why's it happening now?" Probably because there's a lesson somewhere in there that The Universe wants you to learn before you are ready to manifest this. Maybe you're trying to manifest a soulmate, but you need to love yourself before you can love someone else. And so your manifesting exercises aren't working. It could be that you're trying to manifest a new job, but The Universe is trying to tell you that you won't be happy with that job.

Identify the lesson and acknowledge it. Thank The Universe for the chance to learn.

3. Surrender

Lastly, to detach from an outcome, you must surrender to the fact that sometimes negative things are going to happen and that's okay. Simple as that.

Manifesting Bitch Kit

Using the workbook sheet below, think of one time you manifested something, but it didn't come to fruition. Use the 3 steps in chapter 12 to detach from the outcome and write down the lesson you learned from this negative experience.

_____

_____

_____

_____

_____

_____

_____

_____

_____

_____

Detach From The Outcome

Chapter 15

RELEASING THE NEGATIVE MANIFESTATION

After learning the lesson, it's time to let it go as though it never happened.

Imagine your thoughts about the negative experience. Imagine those thoughts are all wrapped up in a ball – just a round ball of negative thoughts and shit, dwelling, and all that. Toss the ball away.

It was part of you, and now it no longer serves you. Much like when we release an intention, we must release negative thoughts that could accidentally manifest into our lives.

Releasing works because it shows your trust in The Universe. You trust that even though you had a negative manifestation, that doesn't stop you from believing that the things you want will eventually come into your life.

If it's hard for you to release the negative manifestation, always come back to the visualization of the ball of negative manifestations. "The ball of negative manifestation," if you will.

Manifesting Bitch Kit

In the workbook sheet below, I want you to take the negative manifestation you used in chapter 12. Write it below and tear out the sheet of paper. Throw it away. Release it.

_____

_____

_____

_____

_____

_____

_____

_____

_____

_____

_____

_____

_____

_____

_____

_____

_____

_____

_____

_____

_____

_____

_____

_____

_____

Chapter 16

REDO

Now it's time to redo the whole process. Replace it and start with a new goal/thing/experience you want to manifest. Here are the 3 ways to redo the process.

1. Rephrase the Manifestation

2. Center Yourself

3. Start All Over with a Fresh Start

1. Rephrase The Manifestation

Say you want to manifest the same thing that didn't come to full fruition the first time. Before you redo, rephrase the manifestation. My friend Sarah was trying to manifest a new job. The first time I worked with her, the manifestation didn't come to full fruition, and of course she was frustrated. I had her use the processes in chapter 12 and 13.

Before she could start all over, I told her to rephrase the goal. Instead of saying she wanted a new job. I had her rephrase it; "I want a new opportunity to make money."

She ended up getting paid to post on Instagram, which she loves because it gives her the freedom she wants, and yes, it's a job, but rephrasing it kept her open to receiving.

Rephrasing the manifestation is so important! You must do it. This is because A: sometimes you'll feel negative if you think of that one time you didn't fully get what you wanted.

And B: you'll see the manifestation in a new way. You need a fresh start as it brings a light, new energy. This will raise your vibration so that you manifest it more easily.

2. Center Yourself

Breathe. Seriously. As you redo the process, clear your mind. Think of the steps I've laid out in Part 1:

1. Just Ask the Universe!

2. Fake It 'til You Make It

3. Release It Like You Just Don't Care

4. Receive it, Dude!

Remember the steps and think of which tools you might want to use.

3. Start All Over With A Fresh Start

When you redo the manifestation process, think of it as a whole new manifestation. Fresh start. New eyes. New thoughts! You got this. Once you rephrase the manifestation, center yourself, it's time to start all over.

Manifesting Bitch Kit

Using the workbook sheet below, rephrase your negative manifestation. That's it. Make sure you rephrase it so much so that you don't even think about that time you didn't fully manifest it the first go around.

_____

_____

_____

_____

_____

_____

_____

_____

_____

_____

_____

Manifest it, Bitch

_____

_____

_____

_____

_____

_____

_____

_____

_____

_____

_____

_____

_____

_____

_____

_____

Conclusion

You made it.

You're ready to be a fabulous manifesting honey ready to take on the world! Here are some key takeaways.

The Five Steps

1. Just ask the Universe!

2. Fake It 'til You Make It

3. Release It Like You Just Don't Care.

4. Inspired Action

5. Receive it, Dude!

Take these steps with you wherever you are. Know that you're manifesting things every day. Thoughts are energetic waves, and The Universe responds to those thoughts. Be grateful and try to be in a positive space.

You're Human!

We're all human. I'm human. You're human. But my hope is that you think of this book and the manifestation steps whenever you desire something new. I am your cheer-leader, and manifestation should be a huge part of your life. Keep applying the steps to your life. Stay present. Be mindful with your thoughts. You can't monitor your thoughts 100% of the time but try to whenever you can.

Live The Life Of Your Dreams

My hope is that you live the life of your dreams, that you attain all you want and spread your positivity and joy all around. Tell your friends about manifestation, live the process, breathe it, and take on your life! Even though manifestation is now part of my life, it wasn't always that way. It took a lot of trials and tribulations to get to a place where I felt like I was in control of my own life, and if I could figure it out, you can too! Trust me! You're meant to enjoy this life! Truly!

Share Your Manifestation Stories

And share your stories with me! I'm on Twitter @mehrkdog and on Instagram @ManifestItMary, and I love hearing all of your stories! Share your stories with friends, family, loved ones – tell them that this process works. The more you spread the joy you're feeling, the more joy will come into your life.

I'm so happy you opened this book. Now go manifest the shit out of your dreams!

Manifest it,

Bitch!

About the Author

Mary Mehrkens is a Los Angeles-based writer, manifestation coach, comedian, producer, and pilates instructor — a jack-of-all trades if you will. She regularly performs stand-up at Flappers Comedy Club, The Comedy Store, and The Improv. She's the co-writer and producer of the award-winning short film, *Satisfaction Guaranteed* and recently worked on the ABC series, *The Fix*. Her manifesting journey started shortly after college, and she continues to speak and teach about the powers of the Law of Attraction and how it has changed her life.